Dedicated to anybody who ever made a mistake
—D. G.

Dedicated to the home team—Christy, Noah, Lilah, and Blue
—K. T.

Text copyright © 2011 by Dan Gutman
Illustrations copyright © 2011 by Kerry Talbott

First published in the United States of America in October 2011
by Bloomsbury Books for Young Readers
www.bloomsburykids.com

For information about permission to reproduce selections from this book, write to
Permissions, Bloomsbury BFYR, 175 Fifth Avenue, New York, New York 10010

Library of Congress Cataloging-in-Publication Data
Gutman, Dan.
The day Roy Riegels ran the wrong way / by Dan Gutman ; illustrated by Kerry Talbott. — 1st U.S. ed.
p.   cm.
Summary: A boy's grandfather tells him about the famous Rose Bowl game in 1929 when the University
of California Golden Bears lost after one of their players ran the wrong way down the football field.
ISBN 978-1-59990-494-8 (hardcover) • ISBN 978-1-59990-495-5 (reinforced)
1. Riegels, Roy—Juvenile fiction. [1. Riegels, Roy—Fiction. 2. Football—History—Fiction.
3. Grandfathers—Fiction.] I. Talbott, Kerry, ill. II. Title.
PZ7.G9846Day 2011   [E]—dc22   2010043098

Art created with mixed/digital media
Typeset in Bodoni Six
Book design by John Candell

Printed in China by C&C Offset Printing Co., Ltd., Shenzhen, Guangdong
2 4 6 8 10 9 7 5 3 1 (hardcover)
2 4 6 8 10 9 7 5 3 1 (reinforced)

THE DAY ROY RIEGELS RAN THE WRONG WAY

Dan Gutman

illustrated by Kerry Talbott

BLOOMSBURY

NEW YORK BERLIN LONDON SYDNEY

Oh, it's a battle out there, folks. At the end of the first quarter, neither team has scored.

The Golden Bears drove all the way down to the Georgia Tech 25-yard line before giving up the ball. There are just a few minutes left in the first half, ladies and gentlemen. Stumpy Thomason of Georgia Tech takes the snap and swings wide left. He has some blockers.

But, oh, wait! A gang of Bears comes out of nowhere and flattens him!

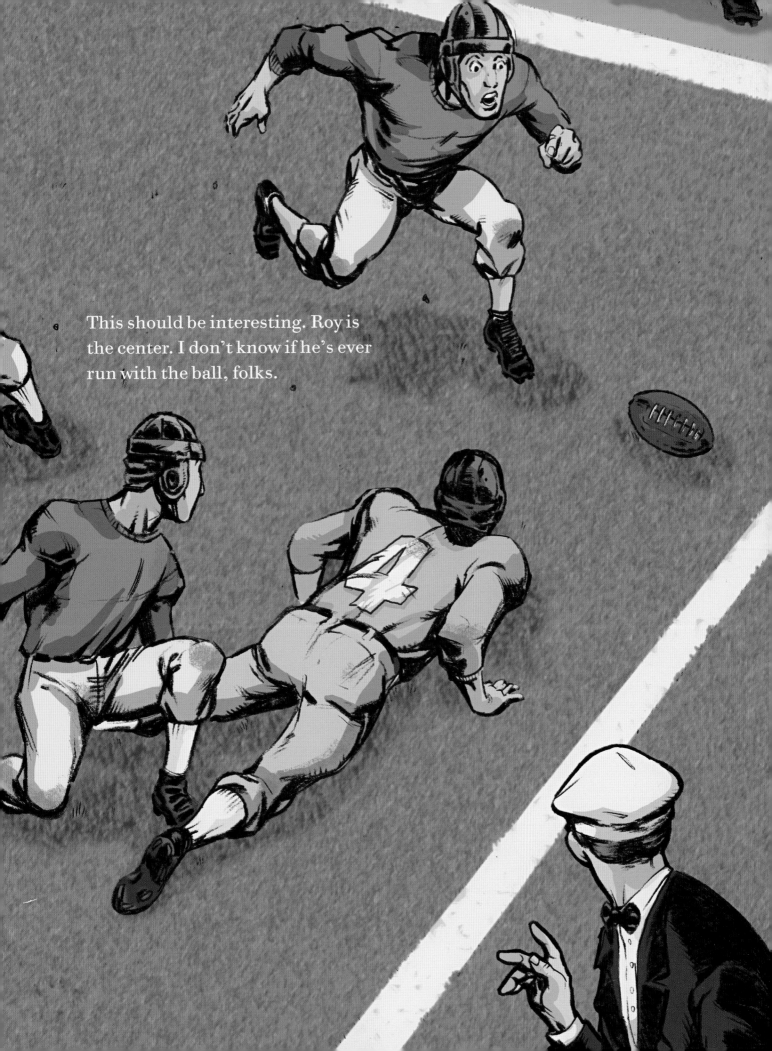

This should be interesting. Roy is the center. I don't know if he's ever run with the ball, folks.

Well, he's running today.
Riegels takes two steps
toward the sideline!
He bounces off one tackler.

He spins away from another.
Riegels sees running room!

Roy is tearing down the sideline like a scared deer!
Nobody is close to him! It looks like he's going to score
a touchdown! But there's just one problem . . .

Wait a minute! Riegels has stopped at the 1-yard line!
It looks like he realizes he ran the wrong way!

Cal has to punt from their own end zone. But here comes Georgia Tech's Vance Maree diving for the ball! He got a hand on it! The ball bounces free! It's rolling out of bounds! That will be a safety!

• A NOTE FROM THE AUTHOR •

This is a true story. The California Golden Bears lost that game 8–7, and Roy Riegels's wrong-way run became one of the most famous moments in football history. But Roy didn't let it get him down. He became the captain of the team the next year. After college, he was a high school football coach. He served in the army during World War II. When the war was over, he started his own fertilizer company. Roy was elected to the University of California Athletic Hall of Fame and the Rose Bowl Hall of Fame.

After a while, Roy was able to laugh about his famous wrong-way run. He even performed it in theaters for people to enjoy. He lived to be eighty-four years old—and for the rest of his life, people called him "Wrong-Way Riegels."